CASEY
AT THE BAT

Library of Congress Number: 84-9891

8 9   97 96 95

Library of Congress Cataloging in Publication Data

Thayer, Ernest Lawrence, 1863–1940.
  Casey at the bat.

  Summary: A narrative poem about a celebrated baseball player who strikes out at the crucial moment of a game.
  1. Baseball—Juvenile poetry.   2. Children's poetry, American. [1. Baseball—Poetry.   2. American poetry]
I. Bachaus, Ken, ill.   II. Title.
PS3014.T3C3   1984   811'.521   84-9891
ISBN 0-8172-2121-2   hardcover library binding
ISBN 0-8114-8357-6   softcover binding

CASEY AT THE BAT

Ernest Lawrence Thayer

Illustrated by Ken Bachaus

RSVP

RAINTREE
STECK-VAUGHN
P U B L I S H E R S
The Steck-Vaughn Company
Austin, Texas

The outlook wasn't brilliant
   for the Mudville nine that day:
The score stood four to two
   with but one inning more to play.

	1	2	3	4	5	6	7	8	9	R	H	E
VISITORS	0	1	0	2	0	0	0	1	0	4	9	1
HOME	0	0	1	0	0	0	1	0		2	7	3

And then when Cooney died at first,
  and Barrows did the same,
A sickly silence fell
  upon the patrons of the game.

A straggling few got up
  to go in deep despair. The rest
Clung to that hope which springs eternal
  in the human breast;
They thought if only Casey
  could but get a whack at that—
We'd put up even money now
  with Casey at the bat.

But Flynn preceded Casey,
   as did also Jimmy Blake,
And the former was a lulu
   and the latter was a cake;
So upon that stricken multitude
   grim melancholy sat.
For there seemed but little chance
   of Casey's getting to the bat.

But Flynn let drive a single,
    to the wonderment of all,
And Blake, the much despis-ed,
    tore the cover off the ball;
And when the dust had lifted,
    and the men saw what had occurred,
There was Jimmy safe at second
    and Flynn a-hugging third.

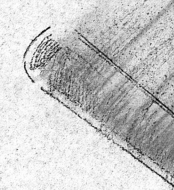

Then from 5,000 throats and more
    there rose a lusty yell;
It rumbled through the valley,
    it rattled in the dell;
It knocked upon the mountain
    and recoiled upon the flat,
For Casey, mighty Casey,
    was advancing to the bat.

There was ease in Casey's manner
   as he stepped into his place;
There was pride in Casey's bearing
   and a smile on Casey's face.
And when, responding to the cheers,
   he lightly doffed his hat,
No stranger in the crowd could doubt
   'twas Casey at the bat.

Ten thousand eyes were on him
as he rubbed his hands with dirt;
Five thousand tongues applauded
when he wiped them on his shirt.
Then while the writhing pitcher
ground the ball into his hip,
Defiance gleamed in Casey's eye,
a sneer curled Casey's lip.

And now the leather-covered sphere
  came hurtling through the air,
And Casey stood a-watching it
  in haughty grandeur there.
Close by the sturdy batsman
  the ball unheeded sped—
"That ain't my style," said Casey.
  "Strike one," the umpire said.

From the benches, black with people,
  there went up a muffled roar,
Like the beating of the storm-waves
  on a stern and distant shore.
"Kill him! Kill the umpire!"
  shouted someone on the stand;
And it's likely they'd have killed him
  had not Casey raised his hand.

With a smile of Christian charity
   great Casey's visage shone;
He stilled the rising tumult;
   he bade the game go on;
He signaled to the pitcher,
   and once more the spheroid flew;
But Casey still ignored it,
   and the umpire said, "Strike two."

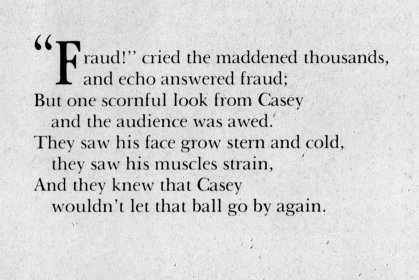

"Fraud!" cried the maddened thousands,
   and echo answered fraud;
But one scornful look from Casey
   and the audience was awed.
They saw his face grow stern and cold,
   they saw his muscles strain,
And they knew that Casey
   wouldn't let that ball go by again.

The sneer is gone from Casey's lip,
   his teeth are clenched in hate;
He pounds with cruel violence
   his bat upon the plate.
And now the pitcher holds the ball,
   and now he lets it go,
And now the air is shattered
   by the force of Casey's blow.

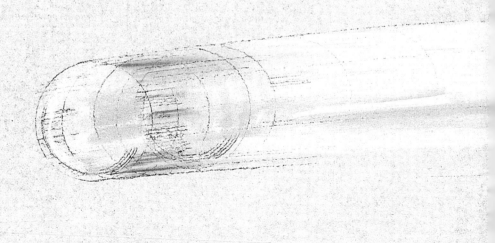

Oh, somewhere in this favored land
   the sun is shining bright;
The band is playing somewhere,
   and somewhere hearts are light,
And somewhere men are laughing,
   and somewhere children shout;

But there is no joy in Mudville—
mighty Casey has struck out.